Wolf Song

Mary Bevis
illustrated by Consie Powell

Raven Productions, Inc 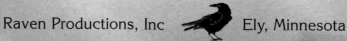 Ely, Minnesota

Text © 2007 by Mary Bevis
Illustrations © 2007 Consie Powell

Published 2007 by Raven Productions, Inc.
PO Box 188, Ely, MN 55731
218-365-3375   www.ravenwords.com

Printed in Minnesota
United States of America
10 9 8 7 6 5 4 3 2 1

Library of Congress Cataloging-in-Publication Data

Bevis, Mary Elizabeth, 1939-
  Wolf song / Mary Bevis ; illustrated by Consie Powell.
    p. cm.
  Summary: At twilight, Nell and her Uncle Walter go into
the north woods, hoping to hear—and join—the howling of
the wolves. Includes facts about wolves and howling
expeditions.
  ISBN 978-0-9794202-0-7 (hardcover : alk. paper) — ISBN
978-0-9794202-1-4 (pbk. : alk. paper)
  [1. Wolves—Fiction. 2. Human-animal communication—
Fiction. 3. Uncles—Fiction.] I. Powell, Consie, ill. II. Title.
  PZ7.B46853Wol 2007
  [E]—dc22   2007027953

For Richard, my husband, who loves the
northwoods as much as I do, and who never
doubted that an answer would come. And to God,
my creator, for the beauty of this earth and for His
continual abundant blessings in my life.

— M.B.

To my neighbors — the furry ones, whose songs
come to me from beyond Farm Lake and the North
Kawishiwi River. Thank you for reminding me to
tell your story, too.

— C.B.P.

Nell scrambled into the old pickup.

"You be careful." Grandma
reached in and hugged her.
"Promise you'll stay close to
Uncle Walter."

"She'll be fine, Sis."
Uncle Walter pulled
the door shut.
"Grandmothers,"
he muttered.
"Always worrying
about something."

Uncle Walter steered the truck onto the gravel road. A rising August moon brightened the twilight sky.
Nell peered through the dusty windshield.
"What's that? Back in the woods!"
"You mean the fox?"
The truck bounced along, climbing and dipping, curving and turning. Soft lights glowed from cabins nestled in the woods.

"AHOoooo," Nell practiced.
"Ahoooooo. How do I sound?"
"Like one of the pack, Nell,"
Uncle Walter chuckled.

"Stop! There's a wolf!"
"Naw. That's Buck, Ben Jasper's
dog." The old woodsman kept on
driving. "At night, anything could
look like a wolf."

"Do you think we'll see a wolf?" Nell asked.

"You never know."

The tires crunched along a narrow gravel road winding up a hill. A hard knot was forming in Nell's stomach.

"You're pretty quiet, Nellie. Still want to go?"

"I've been waiting all summer for this," she whispered.

"Okay," said Uncle Walter. "The road ends here." He parked the truck next to a big white pine.

"Is this where you and Grandpa camped when you were young?"

"The very spot."

"Did you ever call to the wolves?"
"Wouldn't have thought of it.
There weren't many wolves around
here in those days. Now and then we
heard them howl."

A white-throated sparrow flitted
from bush to bush. *Old Sam-
peabody-peabody-peabody*, it sang.
Nell slowly opened the door.
"Uncle Walter, were you ever afraid
of being in the woods at night?"
"You betcha," he replied.

"Will the wolves think I sound like them?" Nell asked.

"It's hard to know what wild animals think."

Nell's eyes searched the shoreline and its shadowy underbrush. Ahead, the woods looked as dark as a raven's shadow.

"Come on. Let's follow the trail," Uncle Walter said, leading the way.

The moon cast shadows. Every boulder looked like a bear. Nell wiped her clammy hands on her jeans. She grabbed Uncle Walter's suspenders and tried to step in his boot prints.

SLAP!!!

Nell nearly jumped out of her skin. A beaver surfaced and swam across the lake.

Nell and Walter climbed over rocks, working their way up the hillside. At the top of the ridge, they stopped to catch their breath. Nell looked up. "Ooh!" she gasped. Overhead the heavens glittered with stars ... thousands of stars, millions ... zillions.

"It's so quiet."
"Maybe to your ears,"
said Uncle Walter. "Listen."
A breeze whispered through the
pines. Waves lapped softly
against the shore. A loon
wailed, long and eerie.

"You ready Nell? I'll start and you join in. "oooooooOOOO."
Nell cupped her hands around her mouth. "oooo oooooOoooo" she called. Her voice sounded weak and quivery. "If they're out there, the pack needs to hear you," said Uncle Walter. "Try again."

"ooooOOOOO," Nell called.
Hoo Hoo to Hooooooo! called a barred owl.
"I don't sound like a wolf," Nell said,
"not even a pup!"
"Don't worry," said Uncle Walter.
"It takes a little practice.
Try again, Nell."
Nell took a deep breath
and raised her head.
"ooOOOOOOOOOOOooo,"
she howled.

Nell waited. She searched for the Big Dipper and Polaris, the North Star. And she waited some more.

They're not going to answer ... they probably aren't even around.

A star streaked across the sky, sparked, and disappeared.

No, wait ...

ooooooooooooooooooooo ooo

"A loon?"
Uncle Walter
pressed his
finger to his lips.

"Sh-h-h, wait."

From the forest a single
cry came again.

Nell grabbed Uncle Walter's hand.
"Are we safe?"
"They don't eat people,
remember?"
Nell held her breath and
hoped the wolves remembered.

A deep, long howl joined
the first. They were
joined by another,
and another, until
the whole pack sang.

The wolf song echoed
across the water and
through the forest
until Nell and
Uncle Walter
were
surrounded
by a great
chorus.

The howls faded one by one. A flying squirrel glided from one tree to another. Nell peered into the darkness. In the dim woods a shadow moved.

Nell held her breath
until the shadow
slipped back into the night.

"Uncle Walter."
"Yes," he said.
"That wasn't a dog ..."
"No." Uncle Walter chuckled.
"Can we stay a little longer?"
"As long as you want."

Nell wanted to run, leap,
shout ... sing a special
song – a wolf song.
But she did not stir.

From deep within the woods
came a faint howl.
Nell raised her voice to the starry sky.
Like one of the pack, she sang back.

Nell's song echoed across the
water and rippled through
the forest until both songs
filled the summer night.

Learn About Wolves

Wolves are intelligent, social animals. They live in family groups called packs, which are led by an alpha male and alpha female. Most of the pack members are this pair's offspring from recent years.

In winter, the alpha pair mates. In spring, three to seven one-pound pups are born. Their den is a protected place such as a cave or hollow log, often near a lake or stream. The mother wolf stays in the den with the pups for the first few weeks after they are born. The other pack members hunt individually at this time when small prey animals such as hares and beaver are abundant and easy to catch. They bring food to the mother while she is staying with the pups.

When they are about a month old, the young pups venture out of the den and begin to explore their surroundings. The mother begins to go short distances for hunting. Pack members begin bringing food back to the pups, too.

By mid-summer the pack moves away from the den area to a rendezvous site. Here the pups stay with at least one "baby-sitter" wolf while the others hunt, turning to the larger prey animals such as moose and deer. After a kill, the hunters bring food back to the pups. By late fall, the pups are grown enough to travel with the pack and to learn to hunt.

Wolves have keen senses. On a clear, calm night when sound travels well, humans might hear a wolf howl from a mile away. In the same ideal conditions, wolves can hear a howl from ten miles away. Wolves can hear a small animal, like a mouse, underneath deep layers of snow. A wolf can smell prey that is upwind more than a mile and a half away.

Wolves howl to greet each other and to communicate with each other when they are separated. Different packs howl to one another to help establish territories. Some experts think that wolves howl just for the joy of it. At the rendezvous site, pups begin to join the adult howls with yips, barks, and short, wavering howls.

Wolves communicate with each other in many ways. They use their ears, eyes, mouths, voices, fur, tails, body postures, and wastes to share information and feelings.

Wolves howl most often during January and February, leading up to the mating season, and during August and September when the pups are learning to become pack members.

Howl with Wolves

You may be able to find a howling expedition to join at a nature center in an area where wolves live. Or if you live in or visit such an area, you can take your own family "pack" out to howl. Here are a few suggestions:

Learn where a wolf pack or fresh wolf kill has been seen recently, and plan to go near there for your howl. Or go to a quiet place within the range of wolves and hope that a pack is nearby.

Choose a clear, calm evening in late summer or mid-winter for the best chance of having wolves return your howls.

Go quietly to your chosen area. Often you can howl from a back road or from a boat or canoe. Or you might hike to a likely spot.

Choose an "alpha" leader for your group ahead of time, so that you don't need to talk before you howl. Alpha starts the howl on a low note, getting higher and louder, then ends by dropping down the pitch and volume. Make the howl last about ten seconds.

Wait about thirty seconds. Then Alpha starts again and, one by one, each pack member joins on a different pitch but with the same pattern of getting higher and louder, then dropping off.

Wait. Listen. If there is no answer after five minutes, try again.

If you still get no answer, try again or move to a new location, perhaps higher or in more of a clearing so that your howls will travel farther.

Wolves don't need to think you are a real wolf pack to answer you, as they will respond to dogs, people, and even sirens. But they might be scared off by human noises, so keep conversation and other non-howling noise to a minimum.

You may not get an answer, but you will still have had an adventure!